The Mysterious Gift

Written by Anne P. Roda

Illustrated by Mona Meslier Menuau

To my grandchildren,
Josie and Leo,
and to all children,
everyone is unique, and everyone is
gifted and deserves to shine their light.
Here's to finding your magic!

Once upon a time, there was a little girl named Katrina who was the youngest child of the King and Queen in the Royal Rose family. Her older brother and sisters called her KayTee and teased her all the time.

"No, you can't play croquet with us. You're too clumsy," said one sister.

"No, you can't ride horses with us. You're too small," said the other sister.

"No, you can't go to the party with us. You're too young," said her brother.

4

KayTee sighed. There were no other children nearby to play with, so she spent much of her time playing with the flower fairies in the palace garden. Even there, her siblings laughed at her.

"Stop playing with the flowers," one sister admonished. "You need some human friends!"

One day when KayTee was playing in the garden, her siblings passed by on their way to play croquet.

"Please, please teach me how to play," KayTee begged.

"How would you keep up with us?" her sister demanded.

Her brother laughed. "You are not even as tall as the mallet!"

KayTee felt like she didn't fit into her family at all.
Crying, she ran through the garden, across the
meadow, and all the way to the edge of the dark forest.

She knew not to enter the forest. *You'll get lost and never found*, her siblings had warned her many times.

"I'll show you!" KayTee said out loud and plunged into the woods.

The trees grew thick, and a misty fog blocked out the sunlight. KayTee caught her foot in a vine and, crying, she fell to her knees.

An elder stepped out from behind a tree. "Why are you crying, little one?" she asked. The woman's face was soft and wrinkled, and her voice was kind.

"My sisters and brother don't like me. I don't belong in my family. I'm not special," KayTee said tearfully. "And now I'm lost!"

9

The elder smiled. "I have a gift for you that will make you feel special." And with that, the woman held out a beautifully wrapped gift. "Take it with you. Come child. I'll help you find your way back home."

Once KayTee could see the castle, she thanked the elder and ran the rest of the way by herself.

In her room, KayTee hid the gift away. She didn't want her brother and sisters to find it and ...

She was a little afraid to open it, as well. What did it mean to be special? Did that mean her brother and sisters would tease her even more?

But in the morning, KayTee decided to open the gift. Her eyes widened in surprise. Inside was a beautiful rainbow-colored dress with mirrors, sequins, and sparkling beads sewn into it. She immediately put it on, and it fit as if it had been made just for her!

She heard her sisters in the hall and quickly took off the dress, hiding it under her mattress.

Later that day her mother, the Queen, called her to the main hall. "Tomorrow, I'm sending you to a special party at a neighboring kingdom. Wear one of your best dresses, Katrina, and remember your manners."

KayTee curtsied. "Yes, mother," she replied.

KayTee felt nervous about meeting so many new people. What would she talk about? Would they all tease her like her brother and sisters? She decided to wear the rainbow dress to the party. It was the prettiest dress she owned.

The next day, KayTee put on her new dress. In the mirror, her eyes sparkled with confidence. She smiled and hummed a song and her heart felt light. She ran down the steps to the carriage, eager to try something new!

At the party, KayTee talked easily with the new people she met, joined in the games, and moved gracefully in the circle dances. No one made fun of her.

I feel as if I belong, KayTee thought.

Except once or twice KayTee saw her siblings scowl at her and heard them whisper behind her back.

That night, KayTee had wonderful dreams, but when she woke in the morning...

Her dress was gone!

Then she remembered how her siblings had been at the party. *Were they jealous of all the attention I got? Did they steal my dress last night?*

"Where have you put my dress?" KayTee asked her siblings at breakfast. "I know you took it!"

"What dress?" asked one sister.

"That old thing you wore last night?" asked the other.

"Don't look at me," said her brother. "I certainly did *not* take your dress!"

18

What will I do? KayTee wondered. If she told the Queen, the Queen would want to know where she got the dress. She couldn't tell her mother she had gone into the forest.

KayTee thought and thought and decided to go back into the woods. Maybe the elder could help her.

Once again, when KayTee was deep in the forest, the elder emerged from behind a tree. "What's making you so sad, little one?" she asked.

"I wore my dress to a party. I had such a good time! But when I woke up this morning it was gone," KayTee cried. "I think my sisters took it."

The elder smiled kindly. "How did you feel wearing that dress?"

"Oh! I felt brave and strong. I could talk and dance and play games," KayTee replied. "I made friends at the party," she added. "Can you help me get my dress back?"

The elder smiled. "Your brother and sisters think that they can take away your power by stealing your dress. They are mistaken. The dress I gave you is beautiful, but it only reflects the true beauty inside of *you*." The elder took hold of KayTee's hands. "Now close your eyes and imagine you are wearing your dress. Remember how you felt."

KayTee did as she was told. She pretended she was putting on her dress and saw how it glittered and sparkled all around her. She remembered how light and happy she felt. She began to hum a song.

"Now, go back home and remember it all," the elder told her.

23

When KayTee got home, she took a deep breath and greeted her siblings with a smile.

"Does anyone want to play ball with me?" she asked.

"Aren't you angry with us?" asked one sister.

"Of course not," KayTee answered. Then she kicked the ball so far and ran so fast her sisters and brother had a hard time catching up with her.

"Wow!" they exclaimed. And later that day, they asked KayTee to play croquet.

When KayTee went to sleep that night, the elder in the woods came to her in a dream.

"You see, KayTee, the dress doesn't have the magic! You have the magic! You just need to believe in yourself. Now that you do, you really don't need the dress anymore. Just remember no one can take your power away from you! You *are* special and you *do* belong."

The next morning, when KayTee woke up, her sisters came into her room. They were holding her dress.

"We're sorry, KayTee," one sister said. "This dress is so beautiful and we—"

"We took it," the other sister confessed. "We're sorry."

KayTee smiled. "I have an idea. Let's share the dress and take turns wearing it. I just know it will be a perfect fit for all of us!"

The Mysterious Gift: Questions and Activities

Just like the elder in the story had KayTee close her eyes and remember how she felt wearing her beautiful dress, let's close our eyes and imagine a time when we wore something or did something that made us feel special and believe in ourselves.

When we're done let's share what we wore or did and how it made us feel.

Did imagining a time like this help you feel like you had a special power or magic inside you?

Can you imagine ways that you can use your special power, especially when you aren't sure of what to do or when you feel nervous and anxious or afraid?

Can you share that with someone or write about it?

Would you like to draw or paint a picture of yourself and your special power?

After you draw or paint it, how does it make you feel to see yourself with it?

Can you share that with someone or write about it? You can keep your picture nearby to help you remember it.

For more questions and activities, visit
AnneRodaAuthor.com

About the Author

Anne Roda lives in Seattle, Washington where she enjoys gardening and writing. Before becoming a gardener, she taught Cultural Anthropology and lived and travelled in Asia and Europe. Once she started gardening, however, she connected with the magic and healing powers of nature, which inspired her to write children's stories. She hopes her stories empower young children to believe in themselves and their unique gifts.

For more resources visit
annerodaauthor.com

About the Illustrator

Mona Meslier Menuau is an illustrator from the west of France. The seaside and the Celtic culture she grew up around fueled a passion for tales and folklore that nurtured her imagination as a child and still shows in her work to this day. The sensibilities of her childhood kept intact, she carefully builds dream-like, comforting universes in her art, with the added subtleties of an experienced self-taught artist. Taking inspiration from a wide variety of creators from all around the world (including but not limited to Tove Jansson, Matthew Forsythe, Ghibli or Paul Grimault), Mona is always searching for new ways to learn to improve her craft.

Made in the USA
Monee, IL
25 October 2022

16544222R00021